P9-DWV-356

A Nutty Nutcracker Christmas

by Ralph Covert *and* G. Riley Mills

illustrated by Wilson Swain

chronicle books san francisco

Text copyright © 2009 by Ralph Covert and G. Riley Mills.
Illustrations copyright © 2009 by Wilson Swain.
All rights reserved. No part of this book may be reproduced in any
form without written permission from the publisher.

Book design by Amelia May Anderson.
Typeset in Cloister and Quincy.
The illustrations in this book were rendered in
acrylic, oil, and colored pencil.

Library of Congress Cataloging-in-Publication Data
Covert, Ralph.
A Nutty Nutcracker Christmas / by Ralph Covert and G. Riley Mills;
illustrated by Wilson Swain.
p. cm.
ISBN 978-0-8118-6111-3
I. Mills, G. Riley. II. Swain, Wilson (David Wilson), 1976– ill. III.
Nutcracker Christmas (Musical) IV. Title.
PZ7.C83412Nut 2009
[Fic]—dc22
2008030936

Manufactured in China, May 2009.

10 9 8 7 6 5 4 3 2 1

This product conforms to CPSIA 2008.

Chronicle Books LLC
680 Second Street, San Francisco, California 94107

www.chroniclekids.com

CALGARY PUBLIC LIBRARY

DEC   - 2009

A Nutty Nutcracker Christmas

Music produced by Ralph Covert and Joshua "Cartier" Cutsinger.

Engineered by Joshua "Cartier" Cutsinger. Additional engineering and mixing by Aidas Narbutaitis. Recorded and mixed at Waterdog Records. All songs written by Ralph Covert and G. Riley Mills © 2005 Waterdog Music (ASCAP) except "Don't Say Impossible" written by Ralph Covert © 2007 Waterdog Music (ASCAP).

MUSICIANS

Steve Gerlach: Electric Guitar
Tom "Pickles" Piekarski: Bass
Chris "Bean" Weng: Drums
Steve Wozny: Piano
Andy Baker: Trombone
Matt Lewis: Trumpet
Rich Parenti: Saxophone

Tom O'Brien: Piano on "Christmas Eve in Our House"
Jim Dinou: Electric keyboards on "Don't Say Impossible"
Dave Thornton: Drums on "Don't Say Impossible"

A Nutty Nutcracker Christmas was first
produced by Emerald City Theatre, Chicago, Illinois.

To Rita, Fiona, Jayme, Abby, and Dingbang . . . and the stinky cheese! —R. C.

For Mom and Dad —G. R. M.

For Grandmother
with thanks to Andrea and Amelia
—W. S.

'TWAS THE NIGHT BEFORE CHRISTMAS,
and everyone at the Stahlbaum house was merry. . . until Fritz
Stahlbaum got himself in VERY BIG TROUBLE.

You see, he broke his sister Clara's favorite nutcracker doll.

So Fritz was grounded. And accused of terrible things.

But the worst part of all, the most tragic, the most unfair and
unreasonable part, was that Fritz's favorite video game, Mouse
Hunter 5000, was taken away and locked in the toy closet!

YOU'RE RUINING CHRISTMAS!
THE ONLY THING YOU'RE GOOD AT IS BEING BAD!

THAT'S RIGHT! I'M A NATURAL!

And *then* everyone left to see the *Nutcracker* ballet, and Fritz had
to stay home with the neighbor, boring old Mr. Drosselmeier, who
INSISTED on telling him the story of the Nutcracker, even though
Fritz was not interested AT ALL.

Then Mr. Drosselmeier talked on and on about his niece, Marie,
who was arriving in an hour with her family, to visit for Christmas.
Fritz did NOT care about that!

All Fritz really cared about was the loss of Mouse Hunter 5000. After all, he was THIS CLOSE to reaching Level 22, where he would finally have a chance to conquer the Mouse King.

SHE'S ABOUT YOUR AGE...

Fortunately, Fritz knew where
the key to the toy closet was hidden.
So, when Mr. Drosselmeier went into
the kitchen to make a phone call, Fritz
snuck his video game out of the closet
and PLAYED.

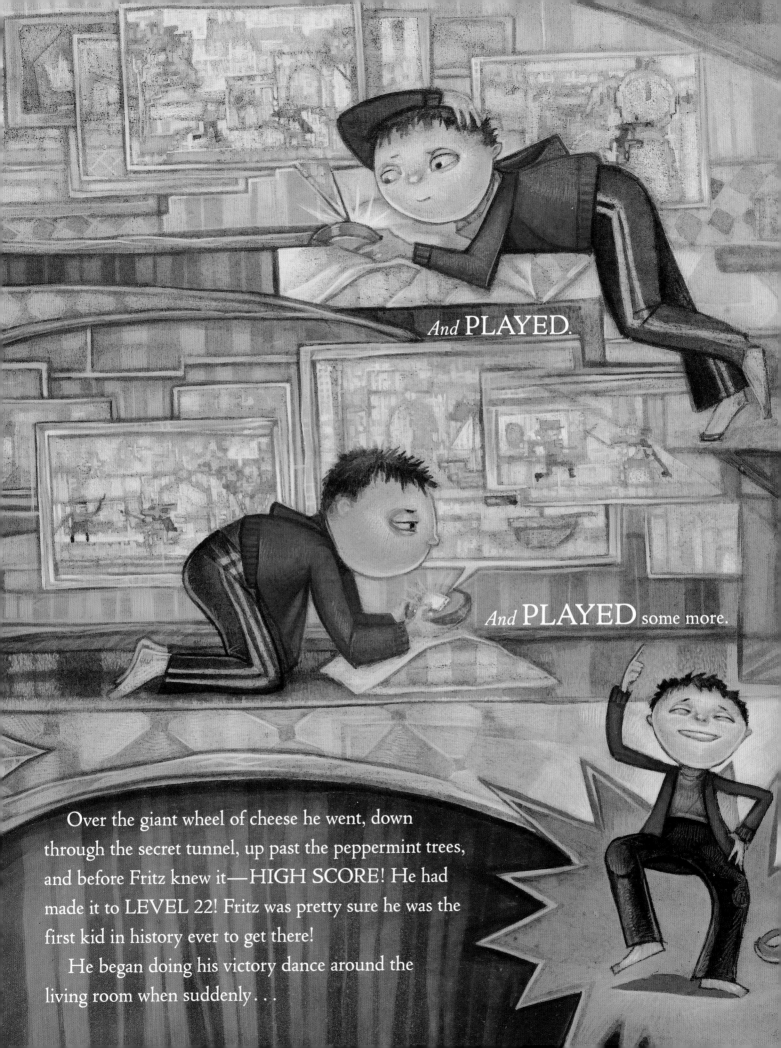

And **PLAYED**.

And **PLAYED** some more.

Over the giant wheel of cheese he went, down through the secret tunnel, up past the peppermint trees, and before Fritz knew it—HIGH SCORE! He had made it to LEVEL 22! Fritz was pretty sure he was the first kid in history ever to get there!

He began doing his victory dance around the living room when suddenly...

. . . he noticed a strange glow coming from inside
the toy closet! Fritz could hardly believe his eyes.
The closet began to rattle and rumble. The door
flew open with a BANG and out came none other than . . .

...THE MOUSE KING himself!

SURPRISE, SURPRISE!

"We meet at last," said the Mouse King, sneering at Fritz and raising his sword. "You've trapped a lot of mice in that nasty video game of yours, but now payback is mine!"

Fritz ducked and dodged, sure he was a goner, when suddenly someone else came bursting out of the closet...

. . . a real live NUTCRACKER!

IF IT ISN'T M

The Nutcracker gave a CHOP!

YOU WON'T GET AWAY THIS TIME, CHEESE BREATH!

A SMACK!

And a KICK!

VORITE NUTCRACKER!

And then the Nutcracker's hat came off,
and Fritz saw something he didn't expect...

DUDE! YOU'RE A GIRL!

DUDE, YOU'RE QUICK...

And just then, the Mouse King slipped back
inside the toy closet and was gone.

"Hurry!" said the Nutcracker to Fritz,
"we've got to catch the Mouse King before he
ruins Christmas!"

An adventure! Fritz liked the sound of that.
So he followed the Nutcracker into the toy closet,
wondering where in the world it would lead.

As they passed through the closet, Fritz
saw a small boat waiting for them at the edge
of an ocean.

"Get in!" said the Nutcracker. "Hurry!"

So Fritz climbed aboard. As they sailed,
the Nutcracker told Fritz all about her
battles with the Mouse King.

"He hates Christmas, because he hates it whenever children are happy," the Nutcracker explained.

"It was me who locked him inside that video game of yours . . ."
"How?" Fritz interrupted.

"Too much to explain now!" the Nutcracker said. "We're here!"

Fritz looked up to see the shore of a strange
and wonderful land.

"Welcome to Christmas Wood!" announced
the Nutcracker with a grin. "Everything here is
made of candy. You can even eat the trees!"

Fritz snapped off a nearby twig—
it tasted like real peppermint!

They sailed along the winding canal through a forest of peppermint trees. There was still no sign of the Mouse King, but Fritz noticed a sea of twinkling lights in the distance.

"That's Toy Town!" smiled the Nutcracker. "It's where Santa's most magical toys come from. We have to get there before it's too late!"

They arrived at the entrance to Toy Town and were greeted by the Mayor of Christmas Wood himself.

WELCOME TO CHRISTMAS WOOD!

SHUT THE GATES FAST!

THE MOUSE KING IS ON THE LOOSE AGAIN,

AND HE'S COMING THIS WAY!

The Mayor quickly ushered them inside, and the large gates closed with a clank.

Toy Town was abuzz with activity. Sugar Plum Fairies flittered about, elves busily wrapped presents, and the town square was filled with the most wonderful toys Fritz had ever seen.

"I'm glad you warned us," said the Mayor. "We were just about to start the Wind-Up Ballet!" "What's *that*?" asked Fritz.

"It happens every year on Christmas Eve," the Nutcracker explained. "It's how the toys say good-bye. You'll see. Follow me to the Gilded Gate!"

The Gilded Gate stood in the center of town, glittering with colorful lights.

"Every toy must pass through this gate before it leaves Christmas Wood," said the Mayor. "The toys here are all alive until that moment. Then the magic goes inside, and only the love of a child can ever bring it out again."

Fritz watched as one of the bears marched through the Gilded Gate and became . . . a *teddy bear*!

Music filled the air as the toys danced with the elves and
fairies, spinning and cartwheeling toward the Gilded Gate.
Everyone was so entranced by the ballet that they didn't notice
the dark figure emerging from the shadows . . .

THE MOUSE KING!

"Looks like I'm just in time," said the
wretched rodent, spraying clouds of nasty,
stinky cheese everywhere.

The Wind-Up Ballet screeched to a halt as
everyone started sneezing and coughing.

Fritz suddenly realized he knew
exactly what to do.

"The blossoms from the peppermint
tree!" He shouted. "Just like my video
game—that's how you get past the
stinky cheese!"

Everyone quickly picked blossoms
from the trees . . . and stopped
sneezing immediately!

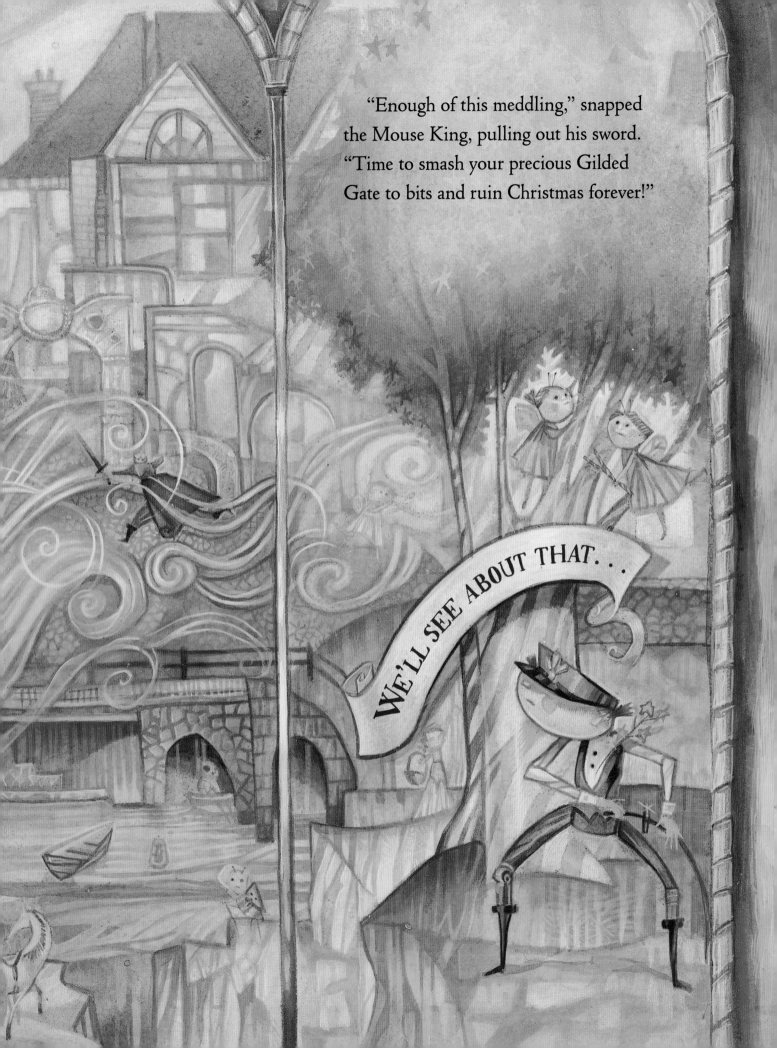

"Enough of this meddling," snapped the Mouse King, pulling out his sword. "Time to smash your precious Gilded Gate to bits and ruin Christmas forever!"

WE'LL SEE ABOUT THAT. . . .

The Nutcracker drew her sword.
"You'll have to get through *me* first."

"With pleasure," hissed the Mouse King.
CLASH! SMASH! "Take that,
you overgrown hamster!"

WHACK! THWACK!

"Oh, no!" cried the Nutcracker as her sword was knocked from her hands. It flew through the Gilded Gate and came out as a toy sword on the other side!

IT'S IMPOSSIBLE TO STOP HIM NOW!

"Looks like it's GAME OVER for you, Nutty!" growled the Mouse King, raising his sword to finish her off.

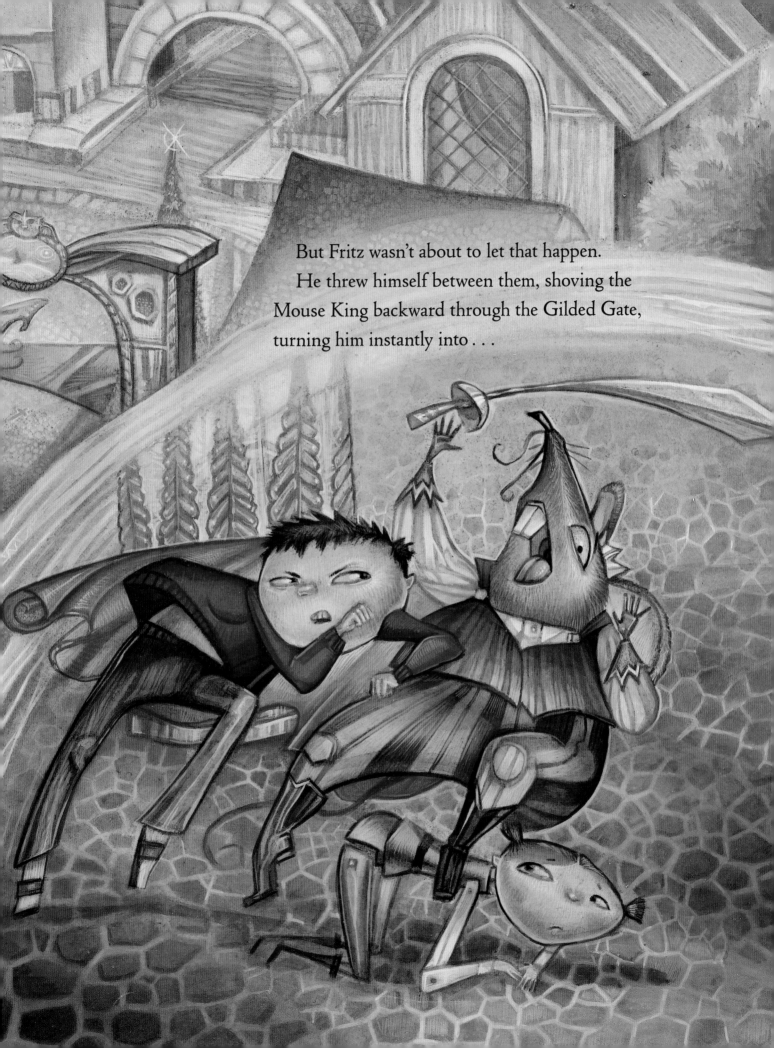

But Fritz wasn't about to let that happen.
He threw himself between them, shoving the
Mouse King backward through the Gilded Gate,
turning him instantly into . . .

"A VIDEO GAME!" cried Fritz.

"And look—the Mouse King is trapped inside!"

"Back where he belongs," said the Nutcracker.
The fairies and elves all cheered with delight.

But there was no time for celebration—they still had work to do!
Fritz and the Nutcracker helped guide each of the toys through the
Gilded Gate as the elves loaded colorful presents onto Santa's sleigh.

Suddenly, bells began to chime.
"It's almost midnight, Fritz," said the Mayor.
"We've got to get you home before Christmas!"
Fritz said good-bye to his new friends. "I'll miss
you all," he said. He saved his last good-bye
for the Nutcracker. "Thank you for
bringing me here!"
The Nutcracker smiled. "Thank
you for helping save Christmas!"

The Sugar Plum Fairies
sprinkled magic fairy dust in Fritz's
eyes making him feel very sleepy. . .

DING-DONG!

The doorbell woke Fritz, at home, in his chair. He rubbed his eyes. Had it all been a dream? It had seemed so real.

"At last! My Christmas guests!" said Mr. Drosselmeier, crossing to the front door. "I told them they could find me here.

In came Mr. Drosselmeier's family, one by one.

Fritz couldn't believe his eyes. Mr. Drosselmeier's niece, Marie, looked just like . . . the Nutcracker!

Soon Fritz's family arrived home from the ballet with boxes of candies and sweets. Everyone danced and laughed, singing their favorite carols.

And for once, Fritz didn't think about video games. He didn't even think about new ways to tease and torment his sister.

Tonight, all he cared about was the Nutcracker.